D1442945

FURRY AND FLO

capstone
young readers

Furry and Flo is published by
Capstone Young Readers
A Capstone Imprint
1710 Roe Crest Drive
North Mankato, MN 56003
www.capstoneyoungreaders.com

Text and Illustrations © 2015 Capstone Young Readers

Library of Congress Cataloging-in-Publication Data
Troupe, Thomas Kingsley, author.
The voiceless vampire / by Thomas Kingsley Troupe ; illustrated by Stephen Gilpin.

        pages cm. -- (Furry and Flo)

Summary: When a Vane, a vampire who is also a top bounty hunter in Furry's world, captures the boy werewolf, it is up to Flo to find a way to rescue him and send Vane back to the other world.

ISBN 978-1-4342-9645-0 (library binding) -- ISBN 978-1-62370-173-4 (paper over board) -- ISBN 978-1-4965-0174-5 (ebook)

1. Werewolves--Juvenile fiction. 2. Vampires--Juvenile fiction. 3. Bounty hunters--Juvenile fiction. 4. Best friends--Juvenile fiction. [1. Werewolves--Fiction. 2. Vampires--Fiction. 3. Bounty hunters--Fiction. 4. Best friends--Fiction. 5. Friendship--Fiction.] I. Gilpin, Stephen, illustrator. II. Title.

PZ7.T7538Vo 2015

813.6--dc23

                                    2014027318

Artistic effects: Shutterstock/Kataleks Studio (background)

Book design by Hilary Wacholz

Printed in China.
092014
008472RRDS15

THE VOICELESS VAMPIRE

BOOK 5

BY THOMAS KINGSLEY TROUPE
ILLUSTRATED BY STEPHEN GILPIN

TABLE OF

CONTENTS

HOME
WALK

CHAPTER 1

Sneaking out of her new school on the first day hadn't been Flo Gardner's brightest idea. Even she knew that. But it wasn't like she'd had a choice. Not when her best friend, Furry, had needed her help. An army of skeletons on the loose wasn't exactly something Furry could have handled alone — even if he was secretly a werewolf.

Flo wished she could say that battling the Bone Horde was the weirdest thing she'd had to deal with since she and her mom moved to Corman Towers, a huge apartment building in the middle of the city. But strange stuff like that happened all the time. Monsters, such as the Bone Horde, were constantly coming out of the portal crack in the basement laundry room to cause trouble.

Flo was one of the only people who knew about the secret portal and the creepy world it led to — the world Furry had come from originally. Personally, Flo it didn't think it was fair that she and Furry were the ones who had to deal with all the creepy crawlies that came through.

Also not fair? After they'd *both* snuck out of Raimi Elementary on the first day, only *one* of them had gotten caught. And it hadn't been Furry.

So now here she was, paying the price for her crime. Flo had spent every afternoon for the past two weeks helping Janice, the school nurse, tidy up the nurse's office as a punishment.

Flo pulled the paper across a narrow cot and tucked it under the plastic strap that held it in place, getting it ready for the next poor kid who felt crummy at school. Then she changed the pillowcase and laid it at the top of the cot.

"Looking good, Flo," Janice said from behind her.

"Thanks," Flo replied with a small smile. Even though Flo wasn't thrilled with her punishment, Janice had been really nice to her. In fact, she and Flo had kind of become friends.

"Let's call it a day," Janice said. "Thanks for helping me out."

"It's only been a half hour," Flo said. "I thought I had to stay until 4:30."

Janice switched off the lamp at her desk and removed a small purse from a drawer. "You want to stay longer?" she teased. "Maybe help the custodians clean up the lunch room?"

"No," Flo said quickly. The lunchroom was a disaster area when everyone finished eating. "That's okay."

"The sun is starting to set earlier, so I'd rather you get home before it gets too dark," Janice said. "Besides, this is the last day of your two-week sentence."

Flo nodded. "Thanks," she said gratefully. "And sorry again for messing up my first day,"

She hadn't told Janice — or anyone else for that matter — *why* she'd had to leave school. No one would believe her if she told them the truth. And even if they would, Flo had promised Furry she'd never tell anyone else about it.

Even if keeping that secret got her in trouble.

Janice shrugged. "Trouble finds us sometimes," she said. "Trust me, I wasn't always an angel when I was younger."

Flo pulled her hooded sweatshirt on over her head and picked up her Dyno-Katz lunchbox. She never went anywhere without it. "What did you do?" Flo asked.

"Oh, I'll tell you some other time," Janice said with a smile. "Maybe when you're a little older."

Janice put her own coat on and followed Flo out the door. Just outside the nurse's office, Flo spotted Furry waiting for her. He was Flo's only real friend in the city and the first person she'd met when she and mom moved into Corman Towers. She'd quickly learned that Furry, wasn't like other boys. For one thing, he was a werewolf. And he wasn't from Flo's world — Furry had been born in the strange world on the other side of the portal crack. He'd stumbled through as a kid — or rather, a puppy. Curtis, the retired maintenance man who lived in the basement, had found him. Other than Flo, Curtis was the only one who knew Furry's secret.

"Hey, Furry," Flo said as Janice locked up behind them. "You didn't have to wait for me, you know."

"You say that every day," Furry said.

He dusted off his backside as he stood up.

Although the early fall weather was brisk,

he still wore a pair of tattered shorts. Flo

knew he probably didn't mind the chillier

temperatures. Furry's werewolf side tended to

keep him warmer than most humans.

"And every day you don't listen," Flo said.

"I still feel bad," Furry whispered, shrugging. "You got caught, and I didn't. Walking home with you is the least I can do."

"You're faster and sneakier than me," Flo whispered back. "With your werewolf senses, there's no way you'd get caught." She stopped talking as Janice approached.

"You two want a ride home?" Janice asked. "Save you the walk?"

"No, thanks," Flo replied with a smile. "We're fine. We don't live that far."

"Okay, then. Good night, Flo," Janice said. "You too, Ferdinand."

"Good night," Furry and Flo replied.

Once they were outside out on the sidewalk, Furry piped up. "How come you never say yes to a ride, Flo?"

Flo kicked a small rock across the cracked sidewalk. She watched it bounce twice before it fell in the gutter. "I don't want Janice to see where we live," she admitted quietly.

"Why not?" Furry asked, furrowing his brow in confusion. "What's wrong with our house?"

"Our apartment building is freaky," Flo said. "What if she saw some kind of creature running around outside the building that we couldn't explain?"

Furry went quiet, and Flo immediately felt bad. Furry was one of the creatures that'd escaped through the portal crack from his world to live in hers. She'd gotten a glimpse of Furry's world after following an escaped mummy back through the crack, and had quickly learned that as freaky as Corman

Towers could get, it was probably the best place Furry had ever lived.

"It's just . . ." Flo began. "I like living there, don't get me wrong. But the old carpet, the peeling paint, the junky old elevator, the monsters coming out of the crack in the laundry room . . ."

"Hey!" Furry cried. "I came from that crack, you know. You think I'm a monster?"

Flo wished she'd kept her mouth shut. She hadn't meant to hurt Furry's feelings. "I don't think you're a monster," she said, picking her words carefully. "I mean, sure you can turn into a werewolf, but you're different."

"Gee, thanks for reminding me," Furry said, scowling.

Flo knew Furry hated being different. *I can't say anything right*, she thought.

"Corman Towers is my home now," Flo explained. "And whether you believe me or not, I like living here. Mostly because of you."

"Really?" Furry looked up, and Flo swore he blushed a bit. "Thanks."

The two quietly walked the rest of the way. When the Corman Towers apartment building loomed in front of them, Furry stopped dead in his tracks.

"What's wrong?" Flo asked. Furry looked as though he'd seen a ghost.

"Something's not right," Furry said. Flo watched his nose twitch as if he was sniffing the air. "I can feel it."

Flo felt a sudden sense of gloom wash over her. *Not again*, she thought. *I just got out of trouble! But if Furry's senses are right, I have a feeling I'm about to get right back into it.*

LURKER
IN THE
LOBBY

CHAPTER 2

As Furry and Flo entered the lobby of Corman Towers, Furry looked around. He had a worried look on his face.

"What?" Flo asked. "What is it?"

Furry was quiet for a minute, then shook his head. "It's nothing," he said. "It felt like someone was watching us, but I must've imagined it."

"Okay . . ." Flo said. She scanned the lobby but didn't see anything.

The two of them headed for the elevators and took them up to the seventeenth floor, where they both lived. "See you later, Flo," Furry said, opening the door to his apartment across the hall.

Inside, Flo could see Furry's adoptive mother, Mona Babbitt, waiting for him. Farther back in their apartment, a man's voice cried, "Welcome home, boy!"

Flo smiled a little. *No wonder Furry isn't exactly anxious to go back to his own world*, she thought. His adoptive parents were always so excited to see him every day.

It wasn't that Flo's mom wasn't excited; she was just usually working. Sure enough, on their apartment door, Flo found a piece of paper taped beneath the peephole. It was a note, written in her mom's hurried script:

Flo fished the apartment key from her pocket and unlocked the door. Once inside, she made sure to lock the door behind her. Living in Corman Towers, she never knew what might show up — and she didn't need any creepy crawlies sneaking in.

Flo tossed her backpack onto the cluttered kitchen table and opened the fridge. Inside, she found a bowl of ravioli with a piece of plastic wrap over the top. She removed the wrap from the bowl and put it into the microwave.

As her meal rotated slowly and grew hotter and hotter, Flo felt kind of lonely. Mom did the best she could, but things hadn't been easy on either of them since her dad died. It was especially tough lately since Mom had started working crazy hours at Jackie's Fashion House and wasn't always home right after school.

The microwave beeped when her food was ready. Flo pulled it out, found a spoon, and dug in. She cracked her math book and bit into raviolis as she solved problems.

After a while, she lost interest and looked up at the wall. The outdated answering machine they'd dragged from place to place sat a little crooked on the wall near the phone. It was old and clunky, and Flo never understood why they still had it. A small red number "1" blinked to show there was a new message.

Interested in anything other than her math homework, Flo got up and pressed the PLAY button. A familiar voice spoke. *"Hey, sweetie, it's Mom. I stopped home for lunch real quick and did a boneheaded thing. I forgot to drop off the rent check downstairs. Can you do me a huge favor and take it down to the office? It's right there on the table. I'll be home a little later, hopefully before you hop in bed. Okay, Flo-tastic. I love you."*

The answering machine beeped to signal the end of Mom's message, and then the machine's electronic voice said, "You have no new messages and eighteen saved messages."

Flo turned and scanned the kitchen table. Somewhere in the mess of envelopes and bills was a check — a late check. Flo rifled through the papers until she found a check made out to CORMAN PROPERTIES. She snatched up the check, along with her lunchbox, and headed for the front door.

On her way out, Flo turned on a few lights in the living room and locked the door behind her. As she did, she heard Furry's family laughing from across the hall. Flo was tempted to knock on the door, but didn't. She couldn't bother them just because she was lonely. Besides, she had a job to do.

Flo rode the clunky elevator down to the main floor to the lobby. In one corner, a cluster of chairs surrounded a small table piled with yellowed magazines. A snack machine with the cracked glass panel sat against a nearby wall. Inside the machine, a fluorescent light flickered, creating a strobe light on the cellophane-wrapped treats. Flo suspected the lobby had been nice at one point in time. Probably, anyway.

She walked past the empty seats and glanced over at the entryway. It was already dark outside. Flo approached the rental office. She knew it was closed, but found the mail slot in the scuffed door. Lifting the metal flap, Flo slipped the check in and let the lid close with a squeak.

When Flo turned around, she saw him.

In one of the worn leather chairs sat a man with the palest skin Flo had ever seen. He stared straight ahead with a steady, unblinking gaze. His eyes were almost completely black except for the slivers of white around the edges. His long, dark hair

was pulled back and tied into a ponytail, and his eyebrows were furrowed as if he didn't like what he saw. He wore a gray shirt made from a rough, old-looking fabric and a pair of black pants, muddied at the cuffs. His feet were encased in a pair of dirty boots, with two large metal buckles on each side.

The blood in Flo's veins seemed to freeze on the spot — as did the rest of her body. Her heart was beating fast, and her breath slowed. Something about the man wasn't right, but she was too afraid to look away.

Just then, something touched Flo's shoulder. She screamed.

FURRY
NOSE

CHAPTER 3

"Flo!" a familiar voice said. "What's wrong? It's me!"

Flo turned and looked up into her mom's face. She looked confused and worried, her eyebrows drawn together above her nose. Her work name tag was still pinned to her sweater. Flo stared at her mom for a moment, then hugged her tightly, burying her face in her mother's jacket.

"What's with the screaming?" Mom asked.

"You scared me," Flo whispered. "And that guy over there is seriously creeping me out."

Mom scanned the lobby. "What guy?" she asked. "What are you talking about? There's no one here, Flo."

Flo whipped around. "What do you—" she broke off as she realized Mom was right. The chair the man had occupied was empty. It was as if he'd simply vanished. Flo blinked and shook her head. "He was right there. I swear."

Flo glanced down each hallway, expecting to see him escape. Nothing. The pale stranger was gone.

"Are you sure he was there?" Mom asked, sounding exhausted. "Maybe it was just the lighting playing tricks on you."

"Yeah . . ." Flo said. "Maybe." But deep down, she knew she hadn't imagined it. He'd been there. And she had a sinking feeling she knew where he'd come from — the basement portal.

"Well, either way, he's gone now, right?" Mom smiled, but Flo could tell she was exhausted. "Let's get upstairs. I'm beat."

As they headed toward the elevators, Mom spoke up again. "Did you get my message?"

"Yeah," Flo said, pressing the UP button. "I brought the rent check down."

"Oh, thank goodness," Mom joked. "We'll be able to live here for at least another month."

Flo knew her mom was just joking, but she couldn't smile. And no matter how hard she tried, the chill that ran down her back wouldn't go away.

I need to talk to Furry, Flo thought. *He sensed something bad earlier. Maybe Mr. Pale 'n' Creepy was it.*

Back in their apartment, it took less than twenty minutes for Flo's mom to fall asleep in the old chair. Her dinner sat mostly untouched on a TV tray next to her. Flo pulled the blanket off the back of the couch and spread it out over her mom. It was a chilly fall night in the city, and even with the windows closed, the apartment was pretty drafty.

Flo clicked the TV off and paced silently around the apartment. She needed to think. There were plenty of *interesting* residents in Corman Towers, but even so, the pale stranger from the lobby definitely looked out of place.

Was he ever really there? Flo wondered. *Maybe Mom was right and I did imagine him.*

She closed her eyes for a moment, and almost immediately she saw him again. His dark eyes seemed to see straight through her, and she shuddered.

Flo was used to weird things happening at Corman Towers, but this time seemed different. The pale guy didn't look like a monster . . . but she still couldn't help but think his appearance was somehow tied to the portal crack. She needed Furry. Her little werewolf friend was the best at sniffing out danger . . . literally.

Careful not to wake up her mom, Flo snatched up her Dyno-Katz lunchbox and headed to the apartment across the hall. She felt a little bad interrupting. It wasn't that late, but as soon as she knocked, the laughter inside stopped, and she heard heavy footsteps approach. A moment later, Jorge Babbitt stood in the open doorway.

"Hello, Florence," Furry's father said with his heavy accent.

"It's Flo, Dad," Furry called, appearing by the big guy's side. Furry wore his usual pair of shorts and nothing else. At first Flo had found it weird that Furry was hardly ever clothed. But once he explained how many items of clothing he'd destroyed when he changed into a werewolf, she tried to be a bit more understanding.

"Sorry to interrupt," Flo said.

"It's okay," Jorge said. He smiled broadly, the gap between his two front teeth showing. "The boy was just doing some silly dance inside. It makes us laugh."

"Want to hang out?" Flo asked Furry. She smiled as if nothing was wrong. "I need to show you something."

Furry glanced at his father for permission.

"It's fine," Jorge said. "Fine, fine."

"Be back soon for homework time," his mother's voice called from inside the apartment. "Test tomorrow, Ferdinand."

"Okay!" Furry shouted, squeezing past Jorge and in to the hall. "Be back later!"

When they were alone, Flo dropped the smile. "You need to come to the lobby. Now."

* * *

Once inside the elevator, Flo wasted no time. "Remember how you got a weird feeling on our way home from school?"

"Yeah," Furry said. "But I don't think—"

"You were right," Flo interrupted him. "Something is going on. I just saw this super creepy pale guy in the lobby, staring at me. Not like *normal* pale. Like, scary pale. Do you

think it has something to do with your dad?"
Suddenly an idea hit her. "Wait a minute.
What if it *is* your dad?"

"What?" Furry said. "My dad? Why—"

"The note!" Flo cried. "Remember? The one
that said he was coming for you? I mean, the
guy I saw didn't really look anything like you,
but still. What if it's your dad making good on
that promise from his note?"

Furry shook his head. "We don't have to
worry about that note," he said. "There's no
way my dad would come here."

"Why not?" Flo asked. "If he wants you
back . . ."

Furry shook his head again. "I don't think
that's what he wants."

Flo was about to ask why when the old
elevator dinged to signal their arrival on the

main floor. The doors swished open, but Flo was afraid to step outside. She stuck her head out cautiously.

Furry shook his head at her scaredy-cat antics. "Really?" he said. "We've battled mummies, giant spiders, goblins, and an army of skeletons, but some guy who needs a tan scares you?"

"You didn't see him. He was seriously creepy," Flo said defensively. "Besides, you're scared of spiders."

"I'm not *scared* of spiders," Furry insisted. "I just don't like them. At all."

"Whatever you say," Flo said. She took a deep breath and walked into the lobby, determined to prove she wasn't afraid. To her relief, it empty. Whoever the guy was, he hadn't returned.

Flo nodded to the chair in the corner. "He was sitting right there," she said. She wrapped her arms protectively around her Dyno-Katz lunchbox, as if shielding herself. "He was super pale, and he had this really long, dark hair pulled back in a ponytail and—"

Furry suddenly came to an abrupt halt. "Did you say ponytail? Was he kind of thin?"

"Yeah," Flo said, nodding. "Why?"

Furry didn't say anything, but his nose perked up, and he thrust his head forward, sniffing the air like a bloodhound that had caught a scent.

Flo shook her head. Even though she knew her friend could turn into a werewolf whenever he wanted, she couldn't get used to Furry acting like a dog in his human form. She almost expected him to drop to all fours to sniff the ground. "You smell something?" she asked.

"Oh, yeah," Furry said. "It reeks in here. Can't you smell it?"

Flo shrugged. "It smells like an old apartment building. Just like always."

Furry shook his head. "There's something else here," he said. He sniffed closer to the chair. He paused for a moment.

"What? What is it?"

Furry looked over at Flo. "Well, this guy is definitely from my world."

"Of course he is," Flo said with a heavy sigh. "Here we go again."

SCENE OF THE GRIME

CHAPTER 4

"So do you know who he is?" Flo asked. "What does he want?"

"Well, I'm not positive," Furry said. "We should go check out the crack in the basement to be sure."

Furry and Flo headed for the stairwell that would take them to the basement. All the way there, Flo looked over her shoulder to see if the stranger was behind them.

"So?" Flo finally prompted. "Are you going to fill me in or not?"

Furry pushed open the door and sniffed around the dirty old stairs. Flo was glad no one else was around to see her friend acting like, well . . . a werewolf.

Finally Furry stood up. "His smell doesn't exactly give me his name, date of birth, and blood type, but from what you said, I have a pretty good idea."

"Well, tell me!" Flo cried. Even though Furry trusted her with his biggest secret, Flo knew he still kept a lot from her. And she hated being kept in the dark.

"I don't want to scare you," Furry said. "In case I'm wrong."

"Are you serious?" Flo said, crossing her arms.

Furry sighed. "Here's the thing," he started. "It smelled like dirt and rot in the lobby, but I couldn't find a scent trail leading to the chair or away from it. Nothing on these stairs or in the elevator, either. It's like this guy just appeared and disappeared in the chair. Like magic."

"What does that mean?" Flo came closer. She couldn't smell anything, but then again, she didn't have a nose like Furry did. "And what did you mean he smells like rot? Like rotten eggs?"

Furry shook his head. "No, like something dead," he said.

Flo had seen mummies in Furry's world a while back — they were rotten and gross, and she *definitely* didn't like the smell of them. "I don't know," she said as they stepped into the basement hallway. "He didn't look or smell dead to me."

"He might be a different kind of dead," Furry explained, cryptic as ever.

"So do you think he just went away?" Flo asked hopefully.

Furry shook his head. "Probably not," he said. His stomach grumbled. It sounded like a creature growling inside his belly. He put a hand over it as if to quiet it. "And even if he's gone for now, he'll be back."

"Do you think your real parents asked that guy to come get you?" Flo asked. "Like the Goblins Three?"

"That's kind of what I'm afraid of," Furry admitted. "But I don't think they would have sent him just because my dad misses one of his sons."

"*One* of his sons?" Flo asked. Her eyes grew bigger. "Hold up a minute. Does that mean you have —"

"Shhh," Furry hissed, interrupting her and avoiding the question.

Flo was about to tell Furry what she thought of him being so rude, but when she saw him point down the basement hallway, her anger faded. She saw him — the pale stranger from the lobby. Just like before, he seemed to appear out of nowhere.

"That's him," Flo whispered, then covered her mouth. She was afraid any noise would draw the man's attention to them.

"Okay," Furry whispered back. "This isn't good. I definitely know that guy."

Before she could ask any questions, Furry grabbed Flo by the arm, pulling her toward the elevators. He pressed the UP button repeatedly. The old elevator groaned as it descended toward the basement.

Flo glanced back the way they'd come. The pale man had clearly spotted them. His dark eyes were focused on their location, and he was headed their way.

"He's . . . he's coming," Flo stammered. "Furry, he's . . ."

"I know, I know!" Furry said frantically.

Old gears ground and pulleys squeaked within the elevator shaft. The pale stranger stood between them and the stairs. If the elevator didn't arrive soon, they'd be trapped. When Flo looked back again, the pale man had picked up the pace. In moments he would be at their side.

DING.

The elevator arrived and the doors *whooshed* open. Without a moment to lose, Furry and Flo dashed inside. Flo kept her eyes on the elevator doors, and the approaching mystery man, as Furry furiously hit the CLOSE DOORS button over and over.

The man's footsteps crunched on the gritty basement floor. He was closer than ever. After what seemed like forever and two weeks, the elevator doors slid closed.

Just then realizing she'd been holding her breath, Flo exhaled and leaned against the back of the elevator car. Her lunchbox clanged noisily against the wall. "That was close," she said. "Too close. Now will you finally tell me who that creepy guy is?"

"Yeah," Furry said, watching the floor numbers light up above the elevator doors as the car moved. "He's a vampire. And a bounty hunter."

Flo almost let her lunchbox drop in shock.

"His name is Vane," Furry finished. "And he's after me."

JUST
MIST

CHAPTER 5

When the elevator dinged, Flo glanced up and realized where they'd gone past their floor. The elevator had come to a stop on twenty-three. "Wait," she said. "What're we doing? Our apartments are on seventeen!"

Flo reached out to push the button for the right floor, but Furry quickly caught her hand, stopping her. He reached out and hit a different button for a higher floor, then pulled Flo out of the elevator and into the hallway

with him. The doors closed and the elevator squeaked its way skyward.

"We can't go back home. At least not yet," Furry whispered. "If we did, Vane would know which floor we live on."

"How does he even know who you are?" Flo asked. "You were never human in your world, right?" As Flo had learned on her accidental expedition to Furry's world, he could exist only in his werewolf form there.

"I'm not sure," Furry said. "Maybe he can sniff out werewolf. He is a hunter after all."

Flo stepped into the dim light of the twenty-third floor. Several of the overhead lights were burned out, casting parts of the hallway in shadow. She listened, certain she'd hear footsteps in the nearby stairwell. But it was silent. Almost too silent.

Just then, Furry's stomach rumbled loudly.

"Holy socks, that stomach of yours is loud," Flo whispered. "Didn't you eat dinner?"

Furry led her down the hallway. "Yeah, but there's a full moon tomorrow. I can't help being extra hungry."

If that was the case, Flo knew she couldn't blame Furry's stomach for growling. She'd seen what happened during a full moon when she first moved into Corman Towers — Furry turned into a werewolf whether he wanted to or not. And in the days leading up to the full moon, he was like a human garbage disposal. He couldn't eat enough. She even caught him stealing her Popsicles!

"What is this place?" Flo asked, looking around the run-down hallway. "Are we even supposed to be up here?"

"This floor has been vacant for a long time," Furry explained. "Curtis showed it to me so I'd have a place to hide out during the full moon. He said that years ago the owners wanted to fix up the building. But to save money, they remodeled only the levels people lived on. They never got to the higher floors."

"Creepy," Flo whispered, looking around. "It's like it's been abandoned."

Furry stopped in front of an apartment with the number 2308 on the door. There was an old-fashioned keyhole below the doorknob. Flo wondered if Curtis, the retired maintenance guy, had an old skeleton key for the lock.

"Let's hide out in here for a few minutes," Furry suggested. He pushed open the unlocked door.

As soon as they entered the apartment, it was clear that no one had lived there in a long time. The carpet felt gritty beneath Flo's shoes, and the air felt thick and musty. There were cobwebs covering the only items remaining — an old kitchen chair with one of the legs broken off and a long-silent record player.

"Okay, we're safe for a few minutes now, right?" Flo said. "So tell me what's going on. This Vane guy is a vampire?"

Furry's stomach rumbled again — loudly this time. Without being asked, Flo opened her trusty lunchbox and tossed her friend a peanut-butter-and-banana sandwich. By now she knew to pack non-meat sandwiches for Furry — even though he was a werewolf, he was also a vegetarian.

Furry caught the sandwich and tore into it immediately. The peanut butter made it impossible to talk, so he simply nodded instead. When the sandwich was gone, he licked his chops and said, "Yeah, he's a vampire all right. Vane gets paid to hunt down the lost and missing."

Just then the floor creaked, and Flo nearly shot out of her shoes. Furry quickly bolted the door shut. His ears perked up like he was listening closely — and he probably was. Furry's werewolf hearing was amazing. Even in his human form, he could hear things from miles away.

Even though it meant moving closer to the front door, Flo edged closer to Furry. If something happened, she wanted someone to scream with. Flo knew vampires came in all shapes in sizes. At least they did in all the movies and books she'd read. Some were good and actually kind of cute. Vane, Flo decided, was not.

"Do you think your dad sent him for you?" Flo asked. "Does anyone else think that you're lost or missing?"

"I don't think my dad considers me lost or missing," Furry said. "He knows where I am. But he probably isn't very happy that I left the portal between your world and mine open, so maybe that's why he sent Vane. To bring me back and close the portal."

"So what do we do?" Flo asked.

"Well, we can't wait here until morning," Furry said quietly. "We have school tomorrow."

The wood floor squeaked in the hallway, and Furry's ears perked up. He glanced around the empty apartment before turning and heading down a dark hallway toward where the bedrooms likely where.

"This Vane guy can't get in here, can he?" Flo called. "I thought vampires couldn't come into your home if they weren't invited in first!"

Furry didn't answer.

"Can he?" Flo repeated.

"You're right," Furry finally replied. "They can't. But the thing is, this isn't technically our home. Our apartments are a few floors below us."

Flo watched the front door nervously, focusing on the ancient-looking keyhole. Off in the bedroom, she heard a grunt, and metal clanged, followed by another more distant banging sound.

"Flo!" Furry suddenly shouted. "Come on!"

As if on cue, a silvery cloud of mist drifted in through the keyhole. It swirled and grew in size as it gathered near the front door. In seconds, the mist morphed into the shape — Vane.

Flo turned and ran down the hallway. She found Furry in the first bedroom, standing near a vent in the far wall. She ran over, and Furry quickly boosted her up. "Climb through!" he instructed.

With a grunt, Flo pulled herself up the rest of the way and slipped through the rectangular hole in the wall. About three feet in front of her was another opening. She climbed through spider webs and dust and dropped onto an old mattress in a different bedroom. It had to be the apartment next door. A battered vent cover lay next to her on the dingy mattress.

A moment later, Furry landed on the bed, feet first.

"Mist?" Flo said incredulously. "Vampires can turn into mist? How the heck are we supposed to escape that?"

"By running!" Furry shouted. He stood up and tugged Flo through the empty apartment and to the front door.

HUNGRY

CHAPTER 6

Furry and Flo flung open the apartment's front door and ran into the hallway. The entrance to the adjoining apartment — the one Vane was still inside — was still closed. Furry dashed to the elevator and pushed the down button. In no time the passenger car arrived and dinged.

"Forget the elevator," Flo whispered, glancing behind her.

Vane could appear at any moment. "We should take the stairs and make him *think* we took the elevator."

"Good idea," Furry said. He zipped inside the car, hit every button with lightning speed, and jumped back out before the door closed.

Flo silently pushed the metal stairwell door open and clutched her lunchbox close as they descended the stairs as quickly and quietly as they could. As usual, some landings were barely lit with a single, bare bulb, while others were completely dark.

When they reached the seventeenth floor, Furry pushed open the door and peeked out to make sure the coast was clear. Flo cautiously stuck her head out after him. She knew she'd shriek if she saw the vampire bounty hunter waiting for them.

Thankfully, the coast looked clear.

At their apartments, Flo looked at her front door, thankful it didn't have a large keyhole like the apartments on the twenty-third floor. At least that was one less for Vane to vaporize himself through.

"Don't leave your apartment tonight, not with Vane out here," Furry said. "It's not safe. He tracked us to the twenty-third floor, so it won't be long until he figures out where we live. Our homes are the only safe place. It's like there are anti-vampire force fields around them."

"And you're sure about the whole vampires-can't-come-in-unless-they're-invited rule?" Flo asked. "How am I supposed to sleep knowing Vane is running around looking for us? And the mist thing? Super creepy."

"I'm positive," Furry replied. "Vampires are evil, nasty things, but they're bound to a certain set of rules. A home is considered holy ground to them. He can't come in unless he's invited. And besides, it's me Vane wants — not you."

"Sure," Flo said, tapping her neck. "Until he gets hungry . . ."

"You'll be fine," Furry promised. "When the sun is up, he won't bother us anymore. Just get inside, lock the door, and don't invite anyone in."

Flo reached for the doorknob but stopped. She was almost afraid to enter, imagining Vane inside, waiting for her.

Furry seemed to sense the fear behind her hesitation. "If something happens, just yell," he said. "I'll come and help."

Flo turned and smiled gratefully at her friend. "You'll come and save me. But who's going to save you?"

"I don't know," Furry said, scratching his messy hair. "You, I guess."

"Good night," Flo said. "I hope."

"G'night, Flo."

* * *

Flo tucked herself into bed that evening, but she was too worried to fall asleep. Her little koala bear night-light didn't do much to make her feel any better. Every shadow seemed to be a looming figure in the corner, waiting for her to close her eyes.

Where is Vane right now? Flo wondered.

She listened for noise in the hallway. What if Mona or Jorge opened the door and let Vane into Furry's apartment?

She got up twice to peer through the peephole in her apartment's front door. Both times she was afraid she'd see Vane's pale, silent face staring back at her. But there was no one there.

He's probably wandering the halls, waiting for us to come out, Flo thought. *Where is he going to hide tomorrow when the sun comes up? In the basement? Curtis lives down there; will he be safe?*

The ceiling above Flo's room squeaked, and she nearly jumped out of her skin.

"It's fine," she whispered to herself. "It's just someone walking around up there. Probably a neighbor or something."

Out of the corner of her eye, Flo thought she saw the long shadow in the corner move, so she jumped out of bed and flipped the switch to turn on the ceiling light. All the creepy shapes and shadows instantly disappeared.

Flo decided it was probably best to leave the light on. "Just for tonight," she said to herself. Her heart raced in her chest as she climbed back into bed. "Or maybe until we get rid of that vampire."

After what seemed like forever, Flo finally fell asleep.

PLAN
PROBLEMS

CHAPTER 7

On the bus to school the next morning, Flo sat next to Furry. She knew most fourth grade girls wouldn't even talk to a third grader, but Flo didn't care. She rarely made friends when she started at a new school. It was always too hard whenever Mom decided it was time to move again.

Furry gnawed on a breakfast burrito and clutched a small bag of donuts in his other

hand. A jelly ring circled his mouth, and he still had a milk mustache.

"Geez," Flo said. "A little hungry?"

"A lot hungry," Furry said through a mouthful of tortilla, eggs, and cheese. "You have no idea."

Flo couldn't watch him eat. She was afraid she'd get sick at the sight of all that food in his mouth. "No sign of our fanged friend last night?" she whispered.

"You mean Vane? The vampire?" Furry asked, just about loud enough for the whole bus to hear. "Nope."

"Cripes," Flo groaned, covering her eyes. She peeked through her fingers at the rest of the bus. "Keep it down! Do you want everyone to hear?"

Furry looked around at the other students on the bus. Thankfully, most of the kids were wearing headphones or talking with one another. "No one's listening to us," he said. "But to answer your question, no. No sign of him. We're safe until sundown. In the meantime, we have to figure out how to get rid of him."

Flo raised her eyebrows at Furry. "How?" she asked. "Even if we do manage to knock him into the portal crack, won't he just come back? I mean, if he's a bounty hunter, it's his job to bring you home."

"You're right," Furry whispered. "This isn't some dumb giant spider chasing spider eggs back into my world."

"We have another problem too," Furry said. "I'm not going to be able to hide out in my apartment tonight."

Flo was confused for a moment, but then she realized what Furry meant — the full moon. Furry's adoptive parents had no idea their son was a werewolf, so once a month when he was forced to wolf out, Furry snuck up to the roof.

"Oh, man," Flo said, swallowing nervously. "That's not good. We need to come up with a plan. I'll brush up on my vampire facts to get some ideas."

Furry nodded. "Good idea." He seemed lost in thought as he inhaled another donut. Flo had never seen one disappear so quickly.

Even if Furry stays hidden tonight, what about tomorrow or the next day? Flo wondered. *How long can we avoid a bounty hunter vampire like Vane?*

FULL

CHAPTER 8

After lunch, Flo asked her teacher, Mrs. Shamp, if she could go to the library instead of recess. Her teacher was excited by Flo's enthusiasm for reading and wrote a special permission slip for Mr. Rivera, the media-center supervisor.

When she got there, Flo went right to the front desk to get Mr. Rivera's attention. "Hi," she said. "I don't have a lot of time, but I need to find every vampire book you've got."

Mr. Rivera lowered his glasses from the top of his curly, salt-and-pepper hair and smiled. Without even bothering to look the books up, he quickly led Flo through the library. Stopping first to the fiction section, then nonfiction, he found more than twenty books by memory. When Flo had enough, she lugged the stack to an empty table, sat down, and started flipping through them.

How do we get rid of this vampire? Flo wondered, scanning page after page. The books were filled with facts about vampires that she already knew: vampires hate garlic; you can't see a vampire's reflection; vampires have cold, corpse-like skin.

"Gross," Flo said. She opened a book titled *The Legend of the Vampire* next and read about how vampires can turn into mist. The book explained that defeating a vampire is tricky, but exposing it to sunlight will make it burst into flames.

That could be a problem, Flo thought. *We can't risk burning Corman Towers to the ground!*

One of the books talked about staking a vampire through the heart, which would stop it for good, but Flo didn't think she had it in her to do that. It just seemed like it would get really messy.

Flo tapped her lunchbox and looked up at the ceiling. *If only smashing one over the head with my lunchbox worked*, she thought. *It'd be simple.*

Lunchtime was almost over, and Flo still hadn't come up with any new ways to stop vampires, so she decided to check out the three most-useful-looking books. She could read through them more later.

"Find everything you were looking for?" Mr. Rivera asked when Flo returned to the front desk. He scanned the books, then slipped a Raimi Elementary Media Center bookmark inside one of the covers.

"I hope so," Flo said, smiling. "Thanks for your help."

Mr. Rivera probably thought she was reading about the undead bloodsuckers for fun. He had no idea they were real.

And I need to keep it that way, Flo thought.

* * *

As Furry and Flo stepped off the bus in front of their building that afternoon, they both looked up. The late-fall sun was already starting to dip lower in the sky, casting strange shadows on Corman Towers. Before long it would be dark, and the moon would be big and bright in the sky.

"We don't have much time," Flo said, tugging open the front door.

"My mo," Furry said, nodding and chewing his way through the cheese sandwich Flo had given him on the bus. Over the past few days, he'd rarely been without a mouthful of food or something to eat. Every forced full-moon transformation did something to Furry's appetite. The little guy couldn't stop eating.

"What?" Flo asked. She hated it when Furry talked with his mouth full — it was almost impossible to understand him. But he was a werewolf so, what could you do?

Furry swallowed. "I said, 'I know.' So what's the plan?" They paused in the entryway. Even though the sun was still out, Flo wanted to make sure the apartment's lobby was clear of pale, fang-bearing visitors. It was. "Is there a plan?"

"I was sort of hoping you'd have one," Flo said. "Vane is from your world after all."

Furry shook his head. "Sorry," he said. "I've been thinking all day and gotten nowhere. But I can't hide forever. We have to get rid of Vane and make sure he never comes back."

Flo quickly walked across the cracked tile floor to the basement stairwell. "Maybe Curtis can help us," she said. The retired maintenance man who lived in the basement had saved their butts more than once.

They took the stairs to the basement and walked down the dark hallway toward Curtis's apartment. Cranky Curtis was the only one besides Flo who knew Furry's big hairy secret. Flo glanced over her shoulder, almost expecting to see Vane materializing in the hallway behind them.

"We're safe while the sun is out," Furry said. "I'm telling you."

"Yeah, yeah," Flo muttered, knocking on the old apartment door. She noticed for the first time that the doors in the basement had the same old keyhole locks as the doors on the twenty-third floor.

Just then the door opened, and Curtis stood there. His wild, white hair was sticking out in every direction, and his thick glasses were perched on his nose. "Oh, boy," the retired caretaker said. "Anytime you two show up, it's trouble. I was just about to watch my stories."

Flo couldn't help but smile. "Well, you're right about one part . . ." she said. "We are in trouble."

"Vampire trouble," Furry added.

Curtis groaned and tightened the belt on his faded terrycloth robe. His TV blared in the background. "Go to your apartments and don't let him in," he said, sounding distracted. "He'll get bored and go away. Simple."

"It's *not* that simple," Flo insisted. "There's a full moon tonight and—"

"Okay," Curtis interrupted. "Then don't stay home. Mona and Jorge can't see just how furry Ferdinand really gets."

"Do you have any anti-vampire stuff?" Flo asked. "You know, like holy water?"

Curtis looked at her like she had a screw loose. "Not just laying around, no," he replied.

"What about garlic and . . ." Flo was almost afraid to ask. "Stakes?"

Curtis nodded, still half-watching the TV in the next room. "Yeah. Maybe. Let me see what I can drum up. Come back later. I'll have something for you."

With that, the retired caretaker closed the door, leaving Furry and Flo standing in the hallway. It was rude behavior, but Flo let it go. Curtis always seemed crabby, but she knew he was a good guy. He'd found a new home for Furry after all.

"Wow, Flo," Furry said, looking impressed. "Do you really think you could stake a vampire through the heart? That's pretty serious!"

Flo shrugged. "I don't want to," she admitted. "But it might be the only way."

As they walked away from Curtis's door, Furry's stomach growled loudly. Flo pointed at Furry's belly. "Because even if we could find someplace to hide, that stomach of yours would give us away!"

FANGS FOR NOTHING

CHAPTER 9

Flo found another note from her mom stuck to her apartment door when she got to the seventeenth floor. *Looks like Mom's working late again*, Flo thought. But considering what she and Furry had to do, that was probably for the best.

She turned and caught Furry just before he slipped into his own apartment. "Are you going to come back over before it gets dark?" Flo asked. "We'll run to Curtis's apartment to get our vampire-bustin' stuff."

"Yeah, okay," Furry said. His stomach let out another loud, desperate rumble.

"Geez," Flo said. "Maybe eat something too. A lot of something. Vane doesn't need any more help finding you."

"Good point," Furry said. And just like that, he was gone.

Flo headed into her own apartment, which was bathed in an orange glow from the setting sun. In the kitchen, Flo saw there was another message on the old answering machine. She pushed the button to listen as she poured a glass of milk.

"Hi, sweetie, it's Mom," a familiar voice said. *"Working late again tonight, but not this weekend. I promise. We'll find something fun to do. Maybe see a movie? You pick. Anyway, I miss you, and I'm sorry. Thanks for being so*

patient through everything, Flo. See you soon. I love you."

Once the message was done, the machine's electronic voice reminded her there were nineteen saved messages. As Flo sipped her milk, she played the first one. Some guy selling cable TV. Delete. A reminder about an upcoming teacher's conference and that school would be closed. Delete.

Flo deleted eighteen messages, then came to the last one. When the machine announced the date, she looked up in surprise — it was from several years ago. In seconds, another familiar voice spoke through the answering machine.

"Hi, girls," her dad's voice said. "I just left the meeting, and it's looking good. Really good."

"Dad," Flo whispered. Suddenly she understood why Mom kept the old worn-out answering machine.

"They're thinking Dyno-Katz will be huge someday," her dad's recorded voice said, "but they want to start small. Maybe run a short episode after a sitcom until it catches on."

Flo knew her dad likely had been coming out of the Toon Tower Studio offices after his big meeting when he left that message. He'd gone to pitch his Dyno-Katz idea to the studio executives. Flo smiled, thinking about how excited he must have been. He couldn't even wait until he flew back home from the West Coast to tell them how it had gone. Dad had wanted them to know the moment he did that Dyno-Katz would be a real live cartoon someday.

"It's finally happening, and I couldn't have done it without you guys," Dad said. "I mean that. Flo, it's like I always tell you. If there's something in your life you need to do, you do it. Don't let anything stop you."

Flo nodded. "I know, Dad." She whispered as tears leaked from her eyes.

"I'll see you when I get home, girls," Dad said. "I love you both like crazy."

A moment later, the machine beeped. "End of saved messages."

It was just a small piece of her dad, but Flo knew all about holding onto mementos. She ran her fingers along the raised characters on the lid of her Dyno-Katz lunchbox.

Before she could think about it more, there was a knock at the door. Flo hurried over and checked the peephole — Furry.

Flo opened the door, and Furry tumbled in. He had a half-eaten apple wedged in his mouth. He darted around the room like his tail was on fire. He stopped to gobble the rest of the apple — core, seeds, and all.

"What's the matter with you?" Flo asked, quickly closing the door behind him.

"The moon is almost out, and it's not all the way dark yet," Furry gasped.

"We won't have time to get to—"

Before Furry finished, he arched his back. His arms shot out behind him, and in seconds, gray fur exploded across his skin. His nose stretched, his ears grew, and his bare feet morphed into fur-covered paws. Big, sharp teeth replaced his smaller human teeth.

Flo watched in horror as Furry threw his head back. It didn't scare her anymore to see him change into a werewolf. She only hoped

he wouldn't . . .

Furry howled at the top of his lungs. The

few pictures hanging on the walls in the

Gardner apartment rattled. Flo's ears rang.

"Oh, man," Flo said. "I was really hoping

you wouldn't do that."

STEAKED!

CHAPTER 10

Flo poked her head out into the hallway outside her apartment to make sure it was empty. It was. "Clear," she reported back to Furry, still hiding inside.

"Can't we just stay here?" Furry said. "We know Vane can't get into your apartment."

"Yeah, but my mom *can*," Flo pointed out. "And she might not be home yet, but she will be. And it's not going to be easy to explain to her why there's a werewolf in here."

Furry sighed. "Okay, good point. Let's go find Curtis."

As soon as they slipped into the hallway, an uneasy feeling washed over Flo. She held her loaded Dyno-Katz lunchbox close. Out of nowhere, Vane materialized in front of them. Before Flo could even shriek, the bounty hunter ran at them, nearly flying down the hallway. With a grunt, he tackled Furry.

"Furry!" Flo cried. "No!"

Flo watched her friend wrestle with the vampire. Vane pinned Furry down and reached behind his back. A coil of rope woven with shiny silver strands was hooked to his belt. On instinct, Flo raised her lunchbox to bring it down on the vampire's head.

In one swift movement, Vane jerked away, darting the other side of Furry. The lunchbox

swished into thin air, missing Vane by a year. A second later, the rope was unfurled and Furry's left leg was tied.

"Ah!" Furry howled in pain. "Silver!"

Flo didn't know what to do, but she couldn't just stand there and watch Furry get trussed up like a wild animal. In seconds, Vane had his right arm was bound. The little werewolf gnashed his teeth and thrashed around, knocking himself loose for a moment.

But Vane just grabbed his other arm and held him down. All the while, the vampire was silent, his eyes narrowed in concentration.

"Run, Flo, run!" Furry yelled. "Get to Curtis! Before it's too late!"

Flo hated to leave Furry, but knew she was outmatched. With tears in her eyes, she ran for the elevator. She jabbed the DOWN button and glanced back. Furry was up and scrambling toward the other end of the hall. Like a cat pouncing on a mouse, the vampire tackled him again.

The elevator opened and with a wipe of her eyes, Flo went in.

* * *

What felt like ages later, Flo pounded on Curtis's door. He didn't answer right away, so she pounded again — harder this time. From inside, Curtis hollered something she shouldn't repeat. Suddenly the door opened, and without asking, Flo barged into Curtis's apartment. Her eyes were streaked with tears, but she didn't care. She had to stop Vane, and Curtis was her last hope.

"Did you make some stakes?" Flo asked. She had never wanted to stake something so much in her entire life. The thought of her best friend bound up and being dragged back to his world tore her apart.

"Well, I made one," Curtis said. He watched her carefully from behind his thick glasses. "Did you need more than that? I thought Ferdinand was vegetarian."

Flo wiped her eyes and blinked, completely confused. "What about garlic? Do you have some?"

Curtis led her through his cluttered apartment to the small kitchen. Magazines and newspapers were everywhere. The smell of burnt TV dinners made Flo's nose crinkle. She smelled something else.

Garlic.

"Here it is," Curtis said proudly. He held up a giant slab of meat, heavily coated on both sides with off-white powder that Flo recognized — garlic salt.

"A garlic steak," Flo moaned. Her legs wobbled as if ready to collapse in frustration. Curtis was a little strange at times, but this took the cake. Flo knew she had to move. In no time, the hunter and his bounty would reach the portal crack. At this point, she'd take what she could get.

"Okay, thanks," Flo said. She took the steak, and dashed out of Curtis's apartment, running for the laundry room as fast as her legs would carry her.

I SEE YOU

CHAPTER 11

Flo crouched down behind the dryers
in the laundry room, her back to the
troublesome glowing blue crack in the floor.
If something else escaped from Furry's world,
she wouldn't even notice. Flo was too focused
on what was in front of her — saving Furry.
She only had one chance to rescue her friend.
She just hoped it would work.

In seconds, she heard Furry's panicked
voice. There was no turning back now.

"I don't want to go," Furry pleaded near the laundry room door. "Please! Tell my dad you couldn't find me. I'm not hurting anyone by being here!"

There was no response from Furry's captor.

Does he ever say anything? Flo wondered. She took a deep breath. Her hand clutched her weapon in a death grip.

One chance.

As Vane rounded the corner with a trussed-up Furry, Flo stood. She pulled her arm back and swung as hard as she could, slapping the vampire across the face with the giant, garlic-covered steak.

Vane groaned as the thick slab of meat connected with his pale, undead jaw.

The vampire staggered backward from the blow, dropping Furry in the process. Still bound in the silver-laced rope, Furry landed dangerously close to the crack.

For good measure, Flo swung again, this time connecting with back of Vane's head. *Fall in the crack, will ya?* she thought.

Instead, Vane took two steps back, covering his face with his hands. It wouldn't be that easy.

"C'mon!" Flo shouted, tossing the steak at the vampire's feet. She grabbed ahold of the rope binding Furry and pulled the little werewolf across the floor behind her. Flo heard him yelp as he bonked into a washing machine.

"Ow!" Furry howled, struggling within the silver-fibered ropes.

"Sorry," Flo cried. There wasn't much time. Vane was fast and would be on them in moments.

Out in the hallway, Flo spotted the janitor's closet just across the hall from the stairwell. She reached it and yanked the door open. With a gentle shove, she nudged Furry inside. The werewolf whimpered a little.

"Sorry," Flo whispered again.

"Quick, close the door," Furry said. "And lock it."

Flo pulled the door closed behind them and twisted the small lock above the old-fashioned keyhole. The inside of the closet was pitch-black and cramped. Flo banged against something metal. When she reached down, she felt a mop and bucket. A moment later, glass crashed at her feet.

"Maybe be a little quieter," Furry mumbled, still strapped in the ropes. "Unless you want Vane to find us."

"I know, sorry," Flo replied. She set her lunchbox on the ground and reached up. Her fingertips brushed a small string. She pulled the cord, and a dim lightbulb lit the closet.

At her feet, Flo saw the remains of a broken mason jar. Small wood screws were littered among the glass pieces and lid. Flo snatched a sharp shard and cut away at Furry's ropes.

"Hedge clippers would be quicker," Furry suggested, nodding to the wall where garden tools hung from pegs.

"I thought werewolves were strong," Flo said, grabbing the clippers. "Why don't you just break out of these ropes?"

"There's silver woven into the rope," Furry said as Flo cut the ropes binding his hands together. "Silver and werewolves don't mix, remember? It burns a bit."

Flo snipped the remaining ropes, and Furry threw them into the mop bucket.

"Thanks for saving me," Furry said. "I thought I was done for."

"You're welcome, but we're not in the clear yet," Flo said. "If Vane knows we're here, can't he can just turn into mist and slip his way into the closet like he did upstairs?"

"Trapped." Furry looked panicked again. "So what do we do?"

Flo looked up at the mason jars with masking-tape labels across the front. NAILS. SCREWS. WASHERS. They were all neatly arranged and capped with metal lids. Beneath them were rakes, shovels, and a few dingy brooms.

Nothing that looked as though it would help fend off a vampire.

Flo looked and noticed a small gap underneath the door. One more way for Vane to sneak in.

We need something to block the door with, Flo thought, remembering her lunchbox on the floor. "I have an idea," she said, looking at the jars again. "But we have to hurry."

"What else is new?" Furry said.

Flo opened her lunchbox, which she'd packed with four sandwiches and two juice boxes. Flo started pulling the sandwiches from their bags and stuffing them into the gap under the door. Once the sandwiches were gone, the gap was completely blocked.

"Perfect," Flo said, brushing crumbs from her hands.

"Wow," Furry whispered. "Good idea. But what about the keyhole?"

"Part two of my plan," Flo replied. "Boost me up."

Furry lifted Flo up, and she heard him grunt. She didn't think she was *that* heavy. Suddenly she saw Furry's furry ears twitch, and he nodded to the door.

"What's the matter?" Flo asked.

"Vane's right outside the door," Furry whispered, letting out a puppylike whine.

"Perfect," Flo said. She grabbed the mason jar labeled WASHERS and jumped down. When she landed, she peered through the keyhole. Her blood ran cold as she saw a dark eye looking straight back at her.

"Holy socks!" Flo cried. They were trapped. Her plan was their only hope. She quickly twisted the lid off the jar and handed the cap to Furry.

"What're you going to do? Fling washers at him?" Furry asked. "Vampires don't mind that so much."

Flo didn't respond. There was no time to talk. She dumped the washers onto the floor until the jar was empty. When she looked up, Vane's eye was gone.

"He's going to come through!" Furry shouted. He backed up against the wall of the closet, but there was nowhere to go.

A JARRING ESCAPE

CHAPTER 12

"I know!" Flo cried. She watched a small wisp of mist trickle through the keyhole. It was time. With one swift movement, she pressed the empty mason jar flat against the keyhole on the inside of the door and caught the mist in the jar.

In seconds, the jar was filled with the shimmering vampire mist. The glass in her hand grew cold, and when it was nearly full,

Flo grabbed the lid from Furry. She jerked the jar from the keyhole and capped the mason jar, spinning the metal lid nice and tight before any of the mist could escape.

"Whoa," Furry gasped, his hairy jaw hanging open in awe. "How'd you think to do that?"

Flo held the jar up to the light and watched the mist swirl around inside the glass. "I used to catch fireflies back at my old house. Kind of works the same way."

Furry shook his head. "So he's stuck in there?"

"All jammed in here," Flo said. "Hopefully for good."

"Jammed up," Furry said with a laugh. "That's awesome."

"It won't be if he busts out of here," Flo said. "Let's get rid of this thing."

The two friends carefully picked their way over the shattered glass and spilled washers before opening the closet door. Flo grabbed her lunchbox and stepped over the smooshed sandwiches and into the hallway.

Furry and Flo hurried down the hallway to the laundry room. They squeezed behind the dryers and stood at the edge of the blue crack in the floor. The garlic steak rested along the wall, tenderized by Vane's face.

"Do you want to do the honors?" Flo asked her friend.

Furry nodded.

"Okay, but be careful," Flo warned, holding it out. "You drop this and he escapes, vampire Vane will have his fangs in a twist."

Furry took the jar and turned it over in his fur-covered paws. He squinted at the mist inside the jar for a minute before shouting, "If you ever get out of that jar, tell my dad I'm never coming back! No matter what, I'm staying here. This is where I belong. This is my home now!"

And just like that, Furry tossed the Vane-in-the-jar down into the crack and back into his world. The crack absorbed the jar with a loud *WHOOSH*.

"And that's where *you* belong!" Furry shouted after it.

Flo patted Furry's hairy shoulder. "Feel better?" she asked.

"Tons," Furry admitted. "Dang. That felt really good."

Flo watched the crack as it dimmed a little and seemed to shrink. She wondered where it led now. She'd learned during her trip to Furry's world that once the sun set there, the portals between their two worlds shifted — it was impossible to know where you'd end up.

Vane had been lurking around Corman Towers for at least two days, so the portals in Furry's world would have shifted more than once. Flo smiled, wondering where in Furry's world the vampire bounty hunter had landed. She hoped the jar had dropped into a turbulent sea or maybe a garlic factory.

"Won't it just make your dad even angrier that Vane came back without you?" Flo asked.

"Yeah, probably," Furry replied.

Flo didn't know how Furry would take it, but said it anyway. "Maybe he really misses you. If I'd ever run away, my dad would've been heartbroken. Back when he was alive, I mean."

Furry shook his head. "My dad doesn't care about me so much," he said quietly. "He just wants me back so the portal will close."

"What about your brothers?" Flo asked. "You mentioned them before. Maybe they want their missing brother back."

Furry stared at the crack. "I don't think so."

"How do you know?" Flo asked. "Did you get along with them?"

Furry shrugged. "I was the runt of the litter," he said. "And they picked on me a lot. Plus I think they all blamed me for what happened to my mom."

Flo opened her mouth to ask what Furry was talking about, but before she could say anything Furry held up a paw to silence her.

"Before you ask," he said, "I don't want to talk about it right now, okay? I want to enjoy this moment while I can. We beat the best bounty hunter in my world. No one else has lived to say that."

Flo nodded. It had to be difficult to carry so many secrets. *I'm starting to understand why he keeps so many to himself*, she thought.

"Well, your secret is still safe with me," Flo said. "And if you ever want to talk, you know I'll listen."

"Thanks, Flo," Furry said gratefully. "Let's go find someplace to hide out for the rest of the full moon." Just then, his stomach growled again. "And maybe get something to eat."

Flo nodded to the space behind the dryers. "You sure you don't want that steak?"

Furry laughed. "I'm hungry, but I'm not *that* hungry."

THE AUTHOR

Thomas Kingsley Troupe has written more than thirty children's books. His book *Legend of the Werewolf* (Picture Window Books, 2011) received a bronze medal for the Moonbeam Children's Book Award. Thomas lives in Woodbury, Minnesota with his wife and two young boys.

THE ILLUSTRATOR

Stephen Gilpin is the illustrator of several dozen children's books and is currently working on a project he hopes will give him the ability to walk through walls — although he acknowledges there is still a lot of work to be done on this project. He currently lives in Hiawatha, Kansas, with his genius wife, Angie, and their kids.

THE SOLEMN GOLEM

Moments later, Furry and Flo stood in front of the laundry room door, their mouths hanging open in shock. The doorway was wrecked, as if something gigantic had forced its way out of the room. The heavy door hung by a hinge, its metal frame buckled and bent. The surrounding wall had cracked and crumbled.

They slipped out through the giant hole in the garage door and into the alleyway behind the building. The smell of garbage and exhaust hit Flo's nose. She covered her nose and mouth against the odor and turned around, gasping at what she saw.

Something was sitting on an old, rusty dumpster — something *big*.

WANT MORE ADVENTURE?

FURRY AND FLO

6

THE SOLEMN GOLEM

Thomas Kingsley Troupe

FIND IT AT
WWW.CAPSTONEKIDS.COM